Helen Claire
Coln Arbor 2019

EVERYDAY RHYMES FOR
THE UNTAMED MINDS

AMY LOU MILLER

ILLUSTRATIONS BY MELINDA MOEN

SECOND

BOOKS OF LORE

SWAN

Published by Second Swan Press
First Edition 2017
Library of Congress Control Number: 2017934266
ISBN 978-0-692-83629-3

Printed in the United States of America

Based on true stories...

Table of Contents

WILD FLOWERS

I'm going to tell you a very dear story,
So come in close and listen.
It's about a day so warm and so bright,
The sun so proud by its glisten.

My father and I stretched out in the grass
And watched the clouds march by.
Then he turned to me with a serious face
And he looked me right in the eye.

He said, "Son, have I ever told you about
The wildest party I've been to?"
"No, Dad," I said with the shake of my head.
What did Dad get himself into?

"Right here in this field, about your age I was.
I remember the breeze being mild.
The ground was swaying, music was playing.
And the flowers, boy were they wild."

"The flowers were wild?" I asked in reply,
For I've never heard such a fuss.
"Moving and shaking!" my father exclaimed.
Right then the breeze swirled around us.

The ground started swaying, music was playing,
I've never seen petals so riled.
I looked to my dad, what a smile he had.
And the flowers, boy were they wild.

COWBOYS AND IDIOMS

A cowboy once told me I was "Too big for my britches."
But he must need his eyes checked;
I'm not busting through the stitches.

Another also said that he was "Gonna hit the sack."
But when I hit the one he'd brought,
He almost hit me back.

What language are they speaking?
What does it all mean?
Maybe there is something wrong with what's in their canteen.

WHAT ARE THEY ALL SAYING?

WHAT DOES IT ALL MEAN?

*WHY DON'T THEY ALL GIVE UP AND
JUST CALL A QUEEN A QUEEN?*

SEA SNACKS

Is it true what they say about deep in the waves

And what they eat for a snack?

About what makes their suction cups stick to all kinds of stuff.

What makes their ink turn so black?

The tiller, the deck, the mast and the rudder,

All wrapped up in the sails.

Wash it all down with a swig of salt water.

A ship for a snack never fails.

RON

I once met a caterpillar walking slow and low.
He'd pace around and make no sound,
He lived outside my window.

I watched him eat,
Then eat some more.
I even watched him sleep.
One time he crawled right up to me,
I swear my big heart leaped.

Then something terrible happened -
Unimaginable, despicable, mean!
The caterpillar I'd grown to love
Was nowhere to be seen.

"Yoohoo?" I yelled.
"Hello?" I sang.
"Where could you have gone?"
I started to sigh which turned to a cry.
I'd even named him Ron.

Days went by and still no Ron,
I was beginning to lose hope.
Then, what's that? Something tiny appeared,
Just dangling like a rope.

Now this rope wasn't any ordinary rope,
It was more like a very small pouch.
"It just moved!" I yelled out loud,
For this my sister could vouch.

"See what's inside," my sister said,
Then an idea came to mind.
It must be Ron, I thought to myself,
And knocked to see what we'd find.

"Ron, is that you?" I asked in earnest.
It started wiggling faster.
"It must be him!" my sister yelled
And we celebrated with great laughter.

The pouch broke open,
We stared in silence,
My heart began to race.
Then a bright creature swarmed before us,
He nearly missed my face.

"A butterfly!" my sister sang
As she chased it 'round the yard.
How could this be? No how, no way.
My expression grew very hard.

My heart dropped low, my temperature high,
I didn't quite know what to say.
"What'd you do with him?!" so I yelled
And he waved as he flew far away.

WHAT'S IN THE TIN, KEIRA QUIN?

The sun was high, the ground was low,
And between them sat a tin.
It was round and curious, its presence so serious.
It belonged to Keira Quin.

"What's in the tin?" I asked Keira Quin;
Her smile reached the sky.
She took off the lid (I was happy she did)
And sang, "Look, I baked you a pie."

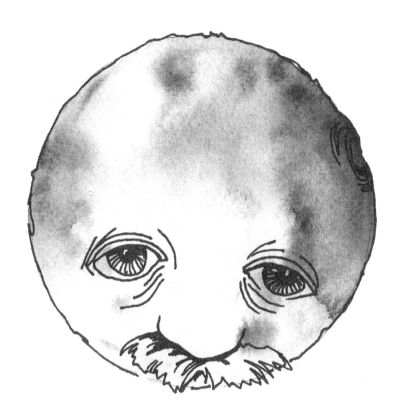

FULL MOON

Why are you so full, oh Moon?
Did you eat yourself to the brim?
I do that, too, sometimes
When I visit my Aunt Kim.

She makes steaks and cakes I just can't save for later.
Braided bread the size of your craters.

How did you get so full, oh Moon?
Did you feast on the rings of Saturn?
We must get you some help, I see
As I fear it's become a pattern.

Some nights you're so slim, just barely a sliver.
The back and forth must be bad for your liver.

I'm sorry you're so full, oh Moon.
Do you have an Aunt Kim?
The greatest downside to being so full
Is waiting an hour to swim.

TO YOU, ON YOUR BIRTHDAY

There really is no map
Of how tall to grow,
And it's truly up to you
To get to where you wish to go.

And while you're on your way,
May the way be so kind.
May you make the best of friends
With the sneaky hands of time.

This road, that road, back roads, no one knows.

Prepare to make some wrong turns before they're right.

You can bloom just like a rose,

But only if you're planted in the light.

Yes, there are highs, and there'll be lows.

And both can call to put up quite a fight.

You can bloom just like a rose,

But only if you're planted in the light.

PLANTS IN THE HOUSE?!

Mother always told me to never track in dirt
Throughout the house
Like some big mouse
That wears my shoes and shirt.

But one day when I walked in
Carefully and clean,
I looked around and what I found
Was simply just so mean.

Plants in the house?
Plants in the house!

But how could this all be?
Maybe what she didn't want
In this house was me.

DEAR ROCK,

POST CARD

HILLS POSTAL
9AM
APR
2016
ONE CENT

Dear Rock,
It's me. This letter's to you.
Why'd you have to take place in my shoe?
Your edges are rough, they're really quite tough.
Don't you have something better to do?

I hope to hear from you very soon.
Right now I'm limping and look like a loon.
Without love,
Me

19

THE FORTUNE TELLER'S DOG

There once lived an old fortune teller,
Who had an old dog he called Keller.
He mixed potions and things, fetched some magical beans.
He turned out to be quite a feller.

Well Keller was not born a dog.
Nor a cat, nor a toad or a frog.
But he came to the teller down in his first cellar...
A fortune that went terribly wrong.

BABY SISTER SINGS THE BLUES

I've got a baby sister cryin',
Can you hear her down the hall?
Oh, my baby sister's cryin',
I can hear her down that hall.
Ain't no way I'm leavin' her lonely.
Out that crib she's gonna crawl.

I've got a baby sister wailin',
Mama better dry those tears.
Oh, my baby sister's wailin',
Mama, please dry all those tears.
I won't ever leave her lonely.
Ooh child, I'll chase off all your fears.

DEAR ME,

CARTE POSTALE

DEAR ME,

IT'S ROCK. I RECEIVED YOUR LETTER.
I REGRET TO INFORM YOU. THERE IS NOTHING BETTER.
WE SEARCH FOR THE BEST SHOE, US ROCKS LIVE TO BUG YOU.
AND WHERE IS YOUR MOM? I'M ABOUT TO UPSET HER...

HI MOM, HAVE YOU NOT WASHED THE SOCKS IN A WEEK?
YOUR SON SURE HAS SOME STINKY FEET.

MY DEEPEST ANNOYANCE,
ROCK

TO THOSE WHO ARE WONDERING...

I've heard the question come up of late
That's been circling around the boys:
If a tree falls and no one's around,
Does that tree falling still make a noise?

Well sometimes my dad makes some funny sounds,

Not quite like a fallen tree limb.

Even when he thinks no one's around

And I'll tell you, *I can still hear him.*

MA, MAKE IT A DOUBLE

It's been a long day, I thought to myself as I sat on the wooden stool.
The sky was cloudy and so was my mood; I'd had a bad day at school.
"What are you drinkin'," my big brother asked as he pulled up a seat next to mine.
I held up my juice box and nodded my head, he took that as a bad sign.
"My homework got lost, the ants won my snack, at lunch I got in trouble."
With a pat on my back he took a deep breath and yelled, "Ma, make it a double!"

The very next day I went out to play then came in to a sorry sight.
My brother was home, he sat all alone and his face just didn't seem right.
Knowing my task I walked up and asked, "What is it, Timothy?"
He quivered his lip and then took a sip and said, "Jenny broke up with me."
My brother once taught me that I really must see the light at the end of the tunnel.
I hopped on the stool, looked at the poor fool and yelled, "Ma, make it a double!"

A YEAR IN THE LIFE

If April showers bring May flowers,
May flowers must have powers.
Powers that flow into June,
Making all that swirly gloom.
Gloom then gets chased from the sky
By the bright sun of July.
Summer sun grants the heat
To bite and nip at August's feet.
Those feet stomp the heat waves down
In time for September to come around.
That's when trees grow wide and tall
And with October starts the Fall.
Fall brings richness to the air
That gives November cozy flair.
This flair burns just like an ember
Bracing for the snow of December.
Then it bows for it must part
As January marks a fresh new start.
Winter cleanses and renews
While February's air stirs right on cue.
March then slips in like a splinter
And Spring then sneaks right up on Winter.
There's beauty in both peace and strife-
This is a year in the life.

BABBLING BROOKE

I have this friend named Brooke and she talks all the time.
She talks about her rabbit's feet and how she'd spend a dime.
She sometimes talks in funny voices, sings her stories through.
She takes no breaths, she takes no prisoners, she talks until she's blue!

Her mother's food, that red balloon, no subject goes untouched.
I even saw her spit one time and that's a bit too much.
I have this friend, her name is Brooke, she talks all the time.

There's something that I must confess...
the name Brooke is mine.

MY DAD'S LAUGH MAKES YOUR DAD LAUGH

My dad laughs so loud, so loud.

HA HA HE HA HA

I heard him once beyond a crowd.

HO HO HE HO HA

Put your ear up to this page
And hold your breath real tight.
I bet you'll hear him laugh so loud,
Just get the timing right.

He's sitting in his favorite chair
And watching favorite shows.
His belly moves, his mouth grows huge.
It crinkles up his nose.

I hear one coming, clear a path!

HA HA HE HA HA

My dad's laugh makes your dad laugh.

HO HO HE HO HA

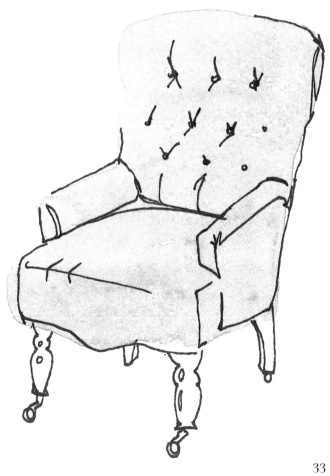

MANNERS YOU MUST MIND

Manners go a long way,
At tables or on streets.
Say your pleases,
Cover sneezes,
Smile at those you meet.

And when you find someday,
Someone leaves all theirs behind;
You still show them
You still know them.
Manners you must mind.

POPSICLE PIONEER

Strawberries, raspberries, cherries and juice.

Chocolate and cinnamon, vibes from a goose.

Laughs and crafts, a couple high fives.

The neighbor's cat and all his nine lives.

Mix it and mix it and mix it some more.

Pour it and juggle to the freezer door.

Waiting and skating, pretending to nap.

Sitting and twiddling thumbs in my lap.

Then, behold! Works of ice appear.

They call me the Popsicle Pioneer.

HA
HA HA
HA HA
HA!

CHOCOL

WILD, WILD VOICES

If the bird, while it flies
Chirps a sweet, artful guise;
Listen up
For the Wild, Wild Voices.

If the ground, as you step
Creaks a sound in protest;
Lend your ears
To the Wild, Wild Voices.

Out in this great earth,
All has its own worth.
No two voices sound the same.
Built just that way
With so much more to say,
And therefore should not dare be tamed.

So the time, it is now.
Find your own to endow.
Let's make peace
With the Wild, Wild Voices.

You were built just that way
With so much more to say,
Let's rejoice
For your Wild, Wild Voices.

CPSIA information can be obtained
at www.ICGtesting.com
Printed in the USA
BVOW11*0226301117

501335BV00022B/252/P